D0714189

SECRET SEVEN

THE SECRET OF OLD MILL

Enid Blyton

THE SECRET SEVEN

THE SECRET OF OLD MILL

Illustrated by Tony Ross

Hodder
Children's
Books

THE SECRET SEVEN

PETER JANET JACK COLIN

GEORGE PAM BARBARA

Have you read them all?

ADVENTURE ON THE WAY HOME

THE HUMBUG ADVENTURE

AN AFTERNOON WITH THE SECRET SEVEN

WHERE ARE THE SECRET SEVEN?

HURRY, SECRET SEVEN, HURRY!

THE SECRET OF OLD MILL

… now try the full-length **SECRET SEVEN** mysteries:

SCAMPER

MIX
Paper from
responsible sources
FSC® C104740

Hodder Children's Books
An imprint of Hachette Children's Group
Part of Hodder & Stoughton
Carmelite House
50 Victoria Embankment
London EC4Y 0DZ
An Hachette UK company

www.hachette.co.uk

CHAPTER ONE

'The secret meeting place can be here,' said Janet, 'in the dark old mill. Nobody ever comes here.'

'Couldn't we go up high in

the old mill?' said Pam. 'There used to be an old stairway that led to a little room.'

Everyone felt excited. They got up and looked for the old stairway. It was a good thing Jack had a torch with him.

Some of the steps were missing. Some were half broken. It was quite exciting to get up them into a dusty, cobwebby, barnlike room above.

This wasn't the little room Pam meant. Peter knew which that was. He took Jack's torch and shone it on to a small, narrow, spiral stairway in one corner. This led up to the tiny room behind the vanes.

The seven children climbed up one behind another.

Peter stood still at the top, barring the way. 'Secret Society Headquarters,' he said. 'Give me the password, please – in a whisper!'

'Tiddlywinks!' whispered Jack.

'Tiddlywinks,' whispered Pam, and they were let in.

The others all remembered the password too, and were soon sitting down in a ring on the dirty floor.

'Usually a Society has a plan for something,' said Janet. 'Something to work for, I mean. What shall we plan?'

'Well, I've got an idea,' said Barbara, sounding rather shy. 'You know that little boy in the village? Well, he's got to

have a big operation but he's
got to go abroad to have it.'

'And we can help raise
the money somehow for the
trip!' cried Janet. 'I think that's
a fine idea for our Secret

Society! I do, really!'

'Well – it would have been nice to plan something more exciting,' said Colin. 'But we can have another plan later. Are we all agreed? Yes, we are!'

CHAPTER TWO

The next time the Secret
Seven met, its members were
very busy indeed! The children
set to work to clean the little
room. The dust was thick and

made them choke as it rose into the air.

When the Seven had finished the job, they put down the old rug that Barbara had brought. It made a very nice carpet in the centre of the little room. Then Janet's stool was set down, and a box that Colin had found down on the ground floor of the mill.

'That's our table,' said

Peter. 'Anyone brought anything for a meal?'

'I've got some cakes that Mummy gave me,' said Pam. 'And Jack's got a whole bag of cherries.'

'And I've got some tarts Mummy made,' said Barbara.

They began to eat the food hungrily. They wished they had thought of bringing something to drink.

'We'd better have a kind of store cupboard somewhere here,' said Jack. 'Then if any of us comes here by himself, and is terribly hungry, he can help himself.'

'Does that mean you're going to visit the Old Mill each day?' said Colin, who knew what a big appetite Jack had. 'If you are, I'm not leaving anything behind!'

'Has everyone finished?' asked Peter. 'Because, if so, we ought to put our earnings into the money box I've brought, and count it up.'

'Yes, we'll do that,' said Janet, and she put an old money box on the table. It belonged to Peter and was in the shape of a pig.

'How much is in the pig?' asked Colin, as each of them

put in his or her bit. Peter was counting as it all went in.

'Goodness – we've put in fifteen pounds and forty pence already!' he said. 'I think that's really marvellous!'

'Have we, really?' said Janet, pleased. 'We'll soon have thirty pounds, then, and probably more by the time the term has ended.'

CHAPTER THREE

It was not long before the
Secret Seven had a nice little
larder up in the tiny room.
It was difficult to eat the
condensed milk without a

spoon, but nobody's mother would allow knives, forks, spoons, or crockery to be taken out of the children's homes. So they had to take it in turns to dip in their fingers and lick them.

'It's really disgusting, of course, eating it like this,' said Barbara. 'I do wish we had spoons and things.'

'I can't think what the

spirit of Old Mill is doing!' said Jack with a grin. 'I told him to provide us with spoons and forks and cups the other day – and not a thing has he produced!'

'Have you all finished?' said Janet. 'If so, I'll clear away.'

She stood on tiptoe to put the things away on the high shelf. As she was pushing a tin to the back, it bumped into something. Janet got the stool and stood on it. She saw a bag at the back of the shelf, and she pulled it out.

'Who put this bag here?' she asked. She **shook** it, and it clinked. She **shook** out the things that were in it. Down they fell on the rug – forks and spoons by the dozen!

Everyone stared in astonishment.

'Spoons – and forks!' said Barbara, in a rather shaky voice. 'Oh, goodness, Jack – the spirit of the Old Mill must have taken you at your word – and sent you the spoons and forks you commanded!'

Well, what an extraordinary thing! But there

were the spoons and forks,
shining on the rug – it was all
perfectly true and real!

CHAPTER FOUR

Barbara and Pam were rather
frightened. As for Jack, he just
made a joke of it.

'Thanks, spirit of the Old
Mill!' he said, and took up a

spoon. 'Very nice of you. What about a few cups now to drink ginger beer in?'

'Oh, don't!' said Pam. 'I'd just hate some cups to come from nowhere.'

'I'll see if there are any put ready for us on the shelf where Janet got these from,' said Jack, and he stood on the stool and felt about at the back of the rather deep shelf.

And he felt something there! Something very heavy indeed – a sack full of things that clinked.

Jack pulled it off the shelf. It was so heavy that when it fell to the ground he was almost pulled off the stool. Without saying a word, Jack undid the rope that tied the neck of the sack. He put in his hand – and brought out a

silver cup! And another and
another – all gleaming and
shining brightly.

'Well – they *are* cups!' he said. 'Sports cups, it is true – but, still, cups. What shall we ask for next? Teapots or something?'

'You're not to talk like that,' said Janet. 'It's making me feel strange. Peter – what do you think is the meaning of this?'

'Well,' said Peter, 'it's nothing to do with Jack's silly

commands, of course. I think that some thieves are using this old mill for a hidey-hole for their stolen goods.'

There was a silence. 'Do you really?' said George. 'Well, I hope they don't come whilst we're here!'

'Shouldn't let them up!' said Peter, at once. 'They wouldn't know the right password!'

'They'd come up just the same,' said Jack.

'I know what we'll do,' said Colin. 'We will come along here late at night and watch to see who the thieves are. That would be a real adventure!'

'Yes!' cried Jack, George, and Peter at once.

'We ought to tell somebody,' said Janet.

'Wait till we find out who the thieves are,' said Peter. 'Then we can go straight along to the police station and tell our great news.'

Chapter Five

At eleven o'clock, Peter was
up in the tiny room in pitch
darkness. A rat scuttled across
the floor and made him jump.
He waited for the others,

wishing they would come.

Ah – *that* was somebody. He waited. No password came. But somebody was coming up the broken stairs. In a panic, Peter stood up quietly in the tiny room far above. Soon whoever it was would be in the room beside him – he would be found by the thieves!

A man came up the spiral stairway and into the tiny

room. He switched on a torch
and went to the shelf. He ran
his torch over the shelf and
then gave an angry grunt.

'Gone! The sacks are
gone! That pest of a Lennie

has been here first. I'll teach him he can't do things like that to me! Wait till I find him!'

Peter kept as still as a mouse whilst the angry voice was going on. Then his heart almost stopped beating. The light of the torch was shining steadily on the pig money box! The thief had seen it.

He picked it up and

shook it. When he heard the money inside, he dashed the pig to the floor and trod hard on it. The pig broke. The money came rolling out.

Peter could have cried to see all their hard-earned pounds and pennies going into the thief's pocket. But he simply didn't dare to say a word.

At last the man went.

Peter hoped the other boys wouldn't run into him! They were very late. The sounds of stumbling down the broken stairs stopped, and there was silence again in the Old Mill.

After a bit, Peter crept out of his hiding place. He almost jumped out of his skin when a word came up the stairs to him.

'**Tiddlywinks**!'

'Pass, brother,' said Peter, thankfully, and up came the other three boys – and behind them came Scamper the spaniel.

Oh, how pleased Peter was to see them all!

CHAPTER SIX

Peter told them all that had
happened. They listened
without a word – and were
very upset when they heard
that their savings had been

stolen from the money box.

'The girls will be miserable!' said Jack. 'I think we've made rather a mess of this, Peter. We ought to have told our parents, or the police, after all.'

'Yes. We ought,' said Peter. 'But I think the second thief will be along soon, because I believe they were to meet here tonight and divide the stolen goods. This fellow thought Lennie, the other thief, had already been here and taken them. He didn't know we had hidden them safely away.'

'I see – and you think we might catch the second thief?' said Jack. 'Right. But I'm not risking anything now – one of us must go to the police station and bring back the policeman!'

'All three of you can go,' said Peter. 'But I'll stay here and watch with Scamper. I'll be safe with him.'

So the three boys set off again in the darkness, leaving Scamper cuddled against Peter's knees in the tiny room above. 'Now, you mustn't make a sound, Scamper,' said Peter. 'Ah – listen – what's that?'

It was a noise down
below. It must be the second
thief. He tightened his hold
on Scamper, who was longing
to growl.

The thief came right up
into the room. He, like the
other man, went to the deep
shelf and found nothing
there. He swept his powerful
torch round the room – and

suddenly saw Peter's feet sticking out from behind the beam!

In an instant, he pulled him out – but he let him go in a hurry when Scamper flew at him. He **kicked** at the dog, but Scamper wouldn't stop trying to **bite** him.

In the middle of all this a voice came up the stairs. The thief heard what it said in the greatest surprise. The voice said: '**Tiddlywinks**,' very loudly indeed.

'**Tiddlywinks**,' said the thief, amazed. 'What does he mean, tiddlywinks?' He went to the top of the spiral stairway and called down. 'Is that you, Jim Wilson? Have you taken the sacks? They're not here – but there's a boy and a dog here. Got to be

careful of the dog!'

'**Tiddlywinks**!' yelled
the voice again. It was Jack,
anxious to know if Peter was
all right.

'Pass, brother!' yelled back
Peter. 'Look out – the other
thief is here. Did you bring a
policeman?'

'Two!' yelled back Jack.
'Nice big ones. Make the
thief come on down. They're

waiting for him.'

The thief was scared. He ran to some rickety steps in the corner of the room. They led up to a tiny attic at the very top of the mill. But Scamper was there before him, **growling**.

'That's right, Scamper! Send him down, send him down!' cried Peter. And Scamper obeyed. He worried

at the thief's trousers, giving
him nasty little nips in the
leg till the man went
stumbling down the spiral
staircase.

Chapter Seven

In the room below were the two policemen, waiting.

'And what about your friend, who helped you to do the robbery?' asked one of the policemen. 'What about Jim Wilson?'

The thief had forgotten that he had called out Jim Wilson's name a few minutes before.

'Jim Wilson's my mate and he lives at Laburnum Cottage,' said the thief. 'He and I did this job together, and we hid the stuff here. We meant to share it. But Jim's

been here first and taken it.
Yes, and hidden it somewhere
safe, too, where you'll never
find it!'

'But we know where it is!'
cried Jack, and he swung his
torch round the room
where they were all standing.

'Look – do you see that
loose board there? Well, we
put the spoons and forks and
cups there, before we left here

tonight! I think they're all solid silver.'

'Yes, they're silver all right,' said one of the policemen, pulling the sacks out of the hole under the

board, and taking out a few of the things.

'The other thief took all our money out of the money box,' said Peter, sadly. 'We'll never get that back, I suppose.'

'He'll have hidden it already, I'm afraid,' said the policeman. He snapped his black notebook shut. 'Well, come along, Lennie. We'll take you away safely and then go

to Laburnum Cottage for Jim.
Nice of you to tell us all about
him.'

'You tricked me!' shouted
Lennie. But his loud voice
made Scamper **growl**

again. 'Call this dog off!' he begged.

Peter called him off. Scamper came back to him, still growling fiercely. Good old Scamper!

'What were you doing here, you boys?' said one of the policemen, as they left the Old Mill and went down the hill.

'Well – we four and three girls often come here,' said

Peter. 'Sort of a meeting place, you know.'

'Oh – you've got a Secret Society,' said the policeman. 'All children belong to one at some time or other. I did myself.'

'Yes,' said Peter, surprised that the policeman guessed so much.

'Tiddlywinks! Ho, that was a password, then?' said

the first policeman, and
he chuckled. 'I must say I
wondered why you boys stood
down there calling tiddlywinks
in the night! Well – your
Secret Society did a lot of

good, didn't it? It's caught us two thieves.'

'Yes. But it's lost us our precious savings,' said Peter. 'We worked hard for that money. We wanted it for Luke – to send him away, you know.'

CHAPTER EIGHT

But a day later something
lovely happened. A letter came
to Peter's house. Inside was
a letter that made Peter and
Janet squeal for joy.

Dear Secret Society,

I hear from the police that you helped them to catch the thieves who stole my silver, and that you hid it in safety when you found it. I am most grateful. Please accept one hundred pounds in gratitude for your Society's good work.

Yours sincerely,

Edward Henry White

'Gracious! That's the man
the silver belonged to!' cried
Peter. 'Mother, look!
One hundred pounds! We can
put it towards sending Luke
abroad for his operation!'

Well, what a surprise! The two rushed off to tell the others the good news, and then off they all went to see Luke. He could hardly believe his good luck.

THE SECRET SEVEN ONLINE

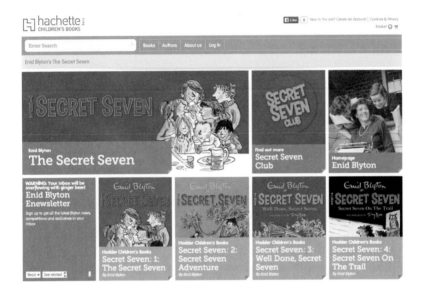

ON THE WEBSITE, YOU CAN:-

- Download and make your very own **SECRET SEVEN** door hanger
- Get tips on how to set up your own **SECRET SEVEN** club
- Find **SECRET SEVEN** snack recipes for your own club meetings
- Take the **SECRET SEVEN** quiz to see how much you really know!

Sign up to get news of brilliant competitions and more great books

AND MUCH MORE!

GO TO ... **WWW.THESECRETSEVEN.CO.UK** AND JOIN IN!

START YOUR
SECRET SEVEN CLUB

In each of the Tony Ross editions of The Secret Seven is a Club Token (see below).
Collect any five tokens and you'll get a brilliant Secret Seven club pack –
perfect for you and your friends to start your very own secret club!

GET THE SECRET SEVEN CLUB PACK:

7 club pencils **7 club bookmarks** **1 club poster** **7 club badges**

Simply fill in the form below, send it in with your
five tokens, and we'll send you the club pack!

Send to:

**Secret Seven Club, Hachette Children's Group,
Marketing Department, Carmelite House,
50 Victoria Embankment, London, EC4Y 0DZ**

Closing date: 31st December 2016

TERMS AND CONDITIONS:
(1) Open to UK and Republic of Ireland residents only (2) You must provide the email address of a parent or guardian for your entry to be valid (3) Photocopied tokens are not accepted (4) The form must be completed fully for your entry to be valid (5) Club packs are distributed on a first come, first served basis while stocks last (6) No part of the offer is exchangeable for cash or any other offer (7) Please allow 28 days for delivery (8) Your details will only be used for the purposes of fulfilling this offer and, if you choose [see tick box below], to send email newsletters about Enid Blyton and other great Hachette Children's books, and will never be shared with any third party.

✂- - - - - - - - - - - - - - - - - - - -

Please complete using capital letters (UK Residents Only)

FIRST NAME:

SURNAME:

DATE OF BIRTH: DD MM YYYY

ADDRESS LINE 1:

ADDRESS LINE 2:

ADDRESS LINE 3:

POSTCODE:

PARENT OR GUARDIAN'S EMAIL ADDRESS:

☐ I'd like to receive a regular Enid Blyton email newsletter and information about other great Hachette Children's Group (I can unsubscribe at any time).

I SECRET SEVEN CLUB TOKEN

www.thesecretseven.co.uk